Little
Leonardo

Julia Hubery ◊ Laura Blakeney

LITTLE TIGER PRESS
London

Leonardo and his teddy were hunting for Useful Things.

"Keep looking, Bob!" said Leonardo. "Today is the perfect day for making Helpful Inventions!"

The friends were searching high and low when they suddenly heard a strange sniffy-snuffling sound.

It was Rabbit! Great big tears were plopping off his whiskers.

"What's the matter, Rabbit?" cried Leonardo, giving his friend a hug.

"I'm a hopeless hopper!" sniffed Rabbit. "I wish
I could bounce a bit bigger."
"How big do you want to bounce?" asked Leonardo.
"As high as the sky!" said Rabbit. "Maybe higher!"
"We'll help!" said Leonardo.

So he and Bob had a little natter,

and a sketch and a scribble.

Then they bashed and
they clattered,

and they tip-tap-jiggled, until . . .

"WOW! Spring-stomping Boing-boots!"
Rabbit beamed. "Thanks, Leonardo – and Bob!"
Rabbit boinged off through the woods.
"Bouncing high, watch me fly!" he sang happily,
when all of a sudden . . .

"Come quickly," Rabbit shouted, "it's Tortoise!"
Poor Tortoise was teetering upside-down,
waving his little legs in the air.

"Thank you!" he said as his friends helped him up.
"I was trying to run, but my legs don't like it. I'll never deliver Aunty Toots's birthday present in time! If only I was whizzier!"

"Don't worry," smiled Leonardo. "We can help."

Leonardo and Bob
nattered and scribbled,

then they tip-tap-jiggled,
until . . .

"Ta-da! Your very own Whizzy-wheeled Skate-banger!" said Leonardo. "You'll be at Aunty Toots's in no time!"

"Thank you, thank you, thank you!" Tortoise cheered. "Fancy a race, Rabbit?"

As the friends sped away, Leonardo and Bob trundled on, searching for Useful Things.

But although they built
a Natty Nut Grabber
for Squirrel . . .

and a Spotty-hankie Floaty-boaty for
Mouse, they didn't find a single
Useful Thing until . . .

Together they huffed and puffed and pulled.

The little cart began to creep very slowly homeward
as the afternoon sun sank lower and lower in the sky.

Soon it was dark. Shadows stretched
out to grab them and the woods whispered
and rustled.

Rabbit froze and shut his eyes. "I'm so
scared!" he quaked.

"Don't worry, Rabbit," said Leonardo.
"I've got a really bright idea this time!"

And with a natter
and a scribble,

and a tip-tap-jiggle, the
beautifully big barbeque
became . . .

. . . "A Star-Bright Night Light," gasped
Rabbit, as a glow of golden stars lit up the
darkness. "Now I won't be scared – we can
walk all night if we have to!"

"But you won't have to!" squeaked a Tortoisey little voice.

"It's Tortoise!" cheered Leonardo. "And Mouse and Squirrel and everyone!"

"We saw the lights!" they cried. "And it's lucky we did – it looks like you need help now, Leonardo!"

Together the friends pushed and pulled,
and the cart rolled happily home,
twinkling all the way.

"Thank you, everyone," said Leonardo as they settled
down with cups of cocoa.
   "And thank YOU for our inventions!" smiled Rabbit.
   "They were whizzy-wonderful!" giggled Tortoise.
   But everyone agreed that the most wonderful
things in the world were truly fantastic friends.